# THE BOY, THE DOLLAR
# AND
# THE WONDERFUL HAT

## STORY BY MARILYN HELMER

## PICTURES BY SAN MURATA

TORONTO   OXFORD   NEW YORK
OXFORD UNIVERSITY PRESS
1992

Oxford University Press, 70 Wynford Drive, Don Mills, Ontario, M3C IJ9

Toronto   Oxford   New York   Delhi   Bombay   Calcutta   Madras   Karachi
Kuala Lumpur   Singapore   Hong Kong   Tokyo   Nairobi   Dar es Salaam
Cape Town   Melbourne   Auckland

and associated companies in
Berlin   Ibadan

Canadian Cataloguing in Publication Data

Helmer, Marilyn
The boy, the dollar and the wonderful hat

ISBN 0-19-540875-6

I. Murata, San, 1940 –   . II. Title.

PS8565.E55B6 1992   jC813'.54   C91-095652-9
PZ7.H45Bo 1992

Oxford is a trademark of Oxford University Press
1 2 3 4 – 5 4 3 2
**Printed in Mexico**

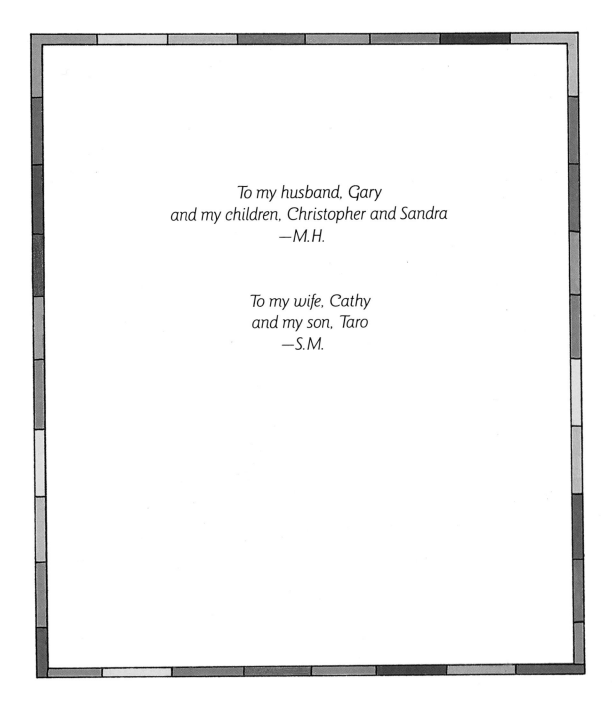

*To my husband, Gary
and my children, Christopher and Sandra
—M.H.*


*To my wife, Cathy
and my son, Taro
—S.M.*

Once a young boy walked to the fair with his father.

When they arrived at the gate the boy's father said, "Benno, here is a dollar for you." He put the money into his son's hand. "Remember now, one dollar will not go far, so spend it wisely. I'll meet you here at four."

Benno was delighted as he waved goodbye. "I will walk around and look at everything," he thought. "Then I will decide what to spend my money on."

At first he walked slowly, taking in the sights and sounds of the fair. He stopped at the vendors' stalls to look at the fascinating array of things for sale. He lingered as his eyes danced over the jumble of hats, balloons, flags and toys. Then the sound of tinkling music caught his ear. Ahead was the midway. Benno walked faster.

Brightly painted wooden animals bobbed and danced on the carousel, begging him to climb aboard. Whirling, twirling rides promised to spin and hurtle him through the air, upside down and downside up. Smells of buttery popcorn, taffy apples and spicy sausages wafted from the food stands. Small, plump ponies stamped the ground, impatient to give rides.

Back and forth Benno walked, his eyes wide with
excitement. Overhead the sun beat down on
the fairgrounds. People strolled by, fanning their
faces, wiping their brows and waving off flies.
Benno saw them, but he was more concerned
with how he would spend his money.

Benno touched the dollar in his pocket. "There
are so many things I want to do," he thought,
"but I can't do everything with only one dollar.
Or can I?" Benno had an idea. His eyes were as
round as his dollar coin. He turned and ran back
to the vendors' stalls.

He found what he was looking for and slapped his dollar down on the counter. "May I have that hat, please?" he asked. He pointed to a wide-brimmed felt hat with silver bells sewn around the bright red band. The vendor handed it to him.

"A good choice, young man," said the vendor with a smile. "This is a wonderful hat. It's not just attractive, it's useful too."

Benno hurried back to the midway. The ticket-taker was standing in the hot sun, wiping his brow and looking very uncomfortable.

Benno offered him his new hat. "If you wear this hat, it will shade you from the sun," he said. "I will lend it to you if you will let me have some rides."

The ticket-taker agreed and put the hat on his head. He smiled at his reflection in a shiny brass pole and decided he looked very handsome indeed.

Benno rode the carousel, the roller coaster, the Ferris wheel, the Scrambler and the Whip. He bumped, looped, whirled and dipped until his stomach and his head seemed to trade places.

By the time he staggered off the last ride, the sun had changed position and the ticket-taker was in the shade.

"This is a wonderful hat," he said, as he handed it back to Benno. "It's not just attractive, it's useful too."

As soon as his head stopped spinning, Benno walked over to the food stands. There he saw a woman behind a tableful of tempting things to eat. She was waving her arms frantically as flies, wasps and bees, attracted by the delicious smells, buzzed over the food. Benno walked up to her and pointed to his hat.

"If you flap my hat at the flies, the jingling bells will scare them away," he said. "I'll lend it to you if you will give me something to eat."

The woman was delighted. She soon found that waving the hat in the air frightened the flies away and attracted customers too. By the time Benno had eaten his fill, the flies were gone and people crowded round the table.

The woman thanked Benno and returned his hat. "This is a wonderful hat," she said. "It's not just attractive, it's useful too."

Benno was tired, but there was one more thing he wanted to do. He headed for the pony rides.

In the field he found a man searching the back of his wagon and muttering to himself. When he noticed Benno standing there he said, "If you want a ride, you will have to wait. My ponies are thirsty and I can't find my water bucket."

"I can help you," said Benno. He pointed to his hat. "If you fill my hat with water, the ponies can have a drink. I'll lend it to you if you will give me a ride."

The man was very pleased. While Benno carried hay from the wagon, the man watered the ponies. Then he insisted that Benno have a ride on each one.

Now the sky had clouded over and a stiff breeze had blown up. By the time Benno had slid off the last pony and patted its nose, his hat was dry.

"This is a wonderful hat," said the man. "It's not just attractive, it's useful too."

Benno thanked the man and reached for his hat. Then he went back to the gate where he was to meet his father.

"What do you think of my wonderful hat?" he asked when he saw his father. "It only cost me a dollar."

His father looked at the hat. "Benno, is this what you spent your dollar on? I thought you would spend it on the rides or the food or the ponies."

Benno turned to his father and grinned. "I had all of those things," he said.

His father stared at him in amazement. "How did you manage that," he asked, "when you spent all of your money on this hat?"

"With this hat I can have anything," answered Benno. I will tell you about it on the way home."

Just then it started to rain. Benno was too tired to walk all the way home, but he had an idea. "Father," he said, "I will help keep you dry, if you will give me a piggyback."

Benno's father laughed and swung him up onto his back. "And how will you do that, Benno?"

Benno reached up and put the hat on his father's head. Then he ducked under the brim. "You see, Father," he said, "this *is* a wonderful hat. It's not just attractive, it's useful too."

And before long, safe and dry, Benno was fast asleep.